"I'm going to kill Jules for setting me up," Kansas said.

"Baby, if anyone was set up, it was me. Sydney knows I'm determined to retire from the Bureau. Throwing you into my bed is no doubt a clever attempt to give me a reason for staying."

"That's ridiculous!"

"I agree. Nothing could make me stay. Not even great sex."

"Rio—"

"I know, I know. I think we're both in agreement about that."

"Which is...?" she asked cautiously.

"Physically attracted, but no interest in pursuing any kind of relationship."

Good. That was exactly how she felt. So why the sudden churning of disappointment in her stomach? "Right. So, what are we going to do? Because this isn't working."

"The way I see it," he said, "we go back in the bedroom, take off our clothes and get rid of the tension so we can concentrate on the job."

Dear Reader,

I hope you've had a warm and cozy holiday season, and are ready to sizzle up the New Year with some fabulous reads from Silhouette Intimate Moments. I sure am!

It's so exciting for me to be able to launch into 2006 with this fast-paced, edgy story. The idea for *Enemy Husband* was born several years ago when I saw the movie *Entrapment* with my own husband. I just loved that opening scene. I wanted my heroine to do that! But yikes, a thief? In an Intimate Moments book....? Sass had better have a darned good reason for stealing that computer disk! And Rio, what can I say? He came out of the shadows, surprising me as much as Sass with his (un)timely appearance. That's the great thing about terrific characters. They really have minds of their own. We authors might think we're in charge, but it's really them....

Enemy Husband will take you on a nonstop thrill ride from Washington, D.C., to the sea islands of South Carolina. Hope you enjoy it! And later this year, please look for my next Intimate Moments book, *Royal Betrayal* (July '06), book 4 of the exciting CAPTURING THE CROWN continuity series, which starts in April.

Good reading!

Nina Bruhns